Amelia Jane
Is Naughty Again!

Enid Blyton™

Amelia Jane
Is Naughty Again!

EGMONT

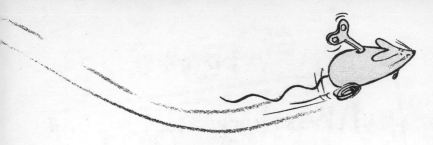

First published in Great Britain 1954 by Newnes
as part of *More About Amelia Jane!*
Reissued 2001 by Egmont Books Limited
239 Kensington High Street, London W8 6SA

ISBN 0 7497 4670 X

10 9 8 7 6 5 4 3 2 1

A CIP catalogue record for this title is available from the British Library

Typeset by Dorchester Typesetting Group Ltd, Dorset

Printed and bound in Great Britain by Cox & Wyman Ltd, Reading, Berkshire

This Edition Published 2007 for Index Books Ltd

Contents

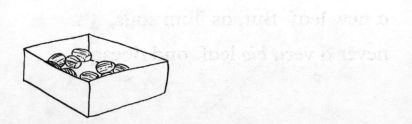

Amelia Jane's Necklace

You remember Amelia Jane, don't you, the naughty doll who lives in the nursery with Tom the toy soldier and the teddy bear and all the other toys?

She's still there – and still naughty, though she does sometimes turn over a new leaf. But, as Tom says, it's never a very *big* leaf, and doesn't seem to last long.

Now, one day Tom went exploring in the toy-cupboard, and he found an old cardboard box. It rattled when he shook it, and he wondered what could be inside.

'Open it and see,' said the teddy bear. So Tom opened it. He and the bear stared at what was inside. They

didn't at all know what the little brown things there were.

'Are they nice big beads?' said Tom.

'They might be something to eat,' said the bear, but he couldn't even nibble a hole in one of the smooth brown things.

The sailor doll strolled up to look. 'Oh, they are *acorns*,' he said. 'Didn't you know *that*?'

'What are acorns?' asked Tom, who had never heard of them in his life.

The sailor doll didn't know, but he pretended to. 'Oh, they are things that can be used for a bead necklace,' he said, remembering that he had once seen the children stringing them together. 'Yes, acorn beads, I suppose. They would make quite a nice necklace, wouldn't they?'

'Oh,' said the bear suddenly. 'Tom, do you think *I* might have an acorn necklace to wear round my neck? Ever since I lost my blue bow I've felt very cold about my neck. I should so like a necklace. It would keep my neck very warm.'

'Well, Teddy, we'll thread you one,' said Tom, who was always very kind. 'Now let me see – what do we want for threading beads?'

'A sharp needle – and some string,' said the sailor doll. 'Look – somebody has already made holes through the acorns, ready for threading. They must have done that and then forgotten all about them.'

Amelia Jane came up, full of curiosity. 'What's that you've got?' she said.

'Acorns,' said Tom, and turned away. He wasn't pleased with Amelia Jane. She had knocked his hat off that morning and pulled out a tuft of his hair to make whiskers for another toy.

'Acorns! What are they?' said Amelia.

'BEADS!' said the sailor doll. 'But NOT for you. For the teddy bear, because he's lost his blue bow.'

'Well, I've lost the lace out of my shoes,' said Amelia Jane. 'I don't see why I shouldn't have the beads as much as the bear.'

'What's losing a shoe-lace got to do with having a necklace?' asked Tom.

'Quite a lot,' said Amelia, who could always argue for hours. 'You see, if I can't have a shoe-lace, I might as well have a neck-lace.'

'Don't be silly,' said the bear. 'You always want everything. Well, you're not going to have *this*!'

The sailor doll, the bear and the toy soldier took the box of acorn beads away to a corner. Amelia Jane

followed them.
They wondered
where to get a
needle and
thread.

'There are
some in the work-
basket,' said Amelia Jane.
Tom climbed up to the
table to get a needle and
some strong thread. He
found a little roll of
string there and
decided that would
do nicely.

Down he came. But, of course,
nobody could thread the little needle

with the thick string.

'Oooh!' said Tom. 'That's the second time I've pricked myself.'

'Bother this,' said the bear, trying hard to push the end of the string through the needle eye. 'It won't go. Oh dear – now *I've* pricked myself!'

'Let *me* try,' said Amelia Jane, and she took up the string. She saw at once that it wouldn't go through the eye of the little needle. She looked at the holes in the acorns. They were big – quite big enough to take the string without a needle to drag it through.

'*I'll* show you!' said Amelia, and she picked up an acorn in her left hand. She ran the string through the hole in it and then picked up another.

'See? Quite easy! You are always so stupid. I'll thread the whole lot now.'

She threaded all the acorns very quickly. She really was clever at things like that.

'Thanks,' said Tom, when she had threaded the whole lot. 'That's fine. Now I'll put the necklace round the bear's neck. It will suit him.'

But Amelia Jane put it round her own! And what is more, she tied the string very tightly into a firm knot. She grinned round at the toys. 'It's mine!' she said, touching the necklace. 'I threaded it, didn't I?'

Well, what was to be done about *that*? Tom was so cross that he held Amelia Jane's arms, whilst the sailor doll tried to undo the knot of the necklace. But he couldn't possibly, because it was much too tight. So they had to give it up and marched off to the toy-cupboard very crossly indeed.

'Mean thing! She's always doing things like that,' said the bear. 'And I did so want a necklace for my throat, now I've lost my blue bow. I do feel upset.'

'It's just like Amelia Jane,' said the sailor doll, gloomily. 'Why didn't we think of her putting it on as soon as she'd finished it? Now we shall never have it, and she'll keep on and on saying, "Look at my beautiful new necklace!"'

That is just what Amelia Jane did say, of course! Whenever anyone came to visit the toys, she would show them her necklace. 'Isn't it lovely?' she would say. 'It's made of acorns. I've heard that they are very, very precious. I made this necklace all by myself!'

Now, that summer was very, very hot. The nursery children went away to the sea, and the toys were left by themselves in the nursery.

'I can't stand this heat,' said

Amelia Jane, one day. 'I'm going out into the garden – and I'm going to undress and get into the pond to cool myself. It's no use saying I mustn't, because I'm GOING to!'

Well, she did, of course. She took off all her clothes except her underwear, which was sewn on and wouldn't come off, and she got into the water at the edge of the garden pond. She lay right down in it, with her head against the edge of the pond, and kicked and splashed in joy.

'It's lovely! It's so cold!' she called. 'Come along and enjoy yourselves, toys! Ooooh! This is delicious!'

The other toys paddled. They were

afraid of undressing and getting right
into the water in case somebody came
in quickly and didn't give them time
to dress and get back to the toy-
cupboard. But Amelia Jane never
cared about things like that.

She spent all day in the water, and
the next day, too, lying there in her
underwear and acorn necklace,

enjoying herself thoroughly. She frightened the sparrows who came to bathe, and she splashed the freckled thrush when he flew down. She really was full of mischief those hot, summer days, and soon no toy liked to go near the pond for fear of being soaked to the skin by Amelia Jane.

Now, if acorns are soaked in water for hours and hours they begin to grow! An acorn is the seed of an oak tree, and if it is made damp, it wants to put out a root and a shoot, like all seeds.

And Amelia Jane's acorns were no different from any other acorns. When they felt the water round them, soaking

into them, they rejoiced, and grew fat.
They wanted to burst their skins, and
put out little white roots and shoots, to
grow into tiny oak-trees!

Nobody noticed that the acorns
had grown fat. Amelia Jane didn't, of
course, because nobody can see what
is tightly threaded round their neck.
But when the acorns burst their skins
a little, and put out white roots, Tom
saw them, and gave a scream.

'What's the matter?' said the bear.

Tom pointed to Amelia Jane's
neck. 'Look! Her necklace is growing
white worms! Ugh, how horrible.
Worms down her neck!'

Everyone stared at Amelia Jane's

neck. She didn't like it at all. 'What's the matter?' she said. 'What's all this about worms?'

'Oh, Amelia Jane – it's quite true. Your necklace has got white worms in it,' said the sailor doll. 'They are wriggling out of the acorns. That's where they live, I suppose! Oooh, how horrible!'

'I don't believe you,' said Amelia, and she put up her hand to her necklace. She touched one or two of the growing white roots and gave a scream. 'Oh, I touched a worm! I did, I did! Oh, whatever shall I do?'

'Well, you *would* take the necklace,' said the bear, quite pleased. 'It's your own fault. You shouldn't have been so selfish.'

Amelia Jane stood trembling in the nursery. 'Will they crawl down my neck?' she said, looking pale.

'I expect so,' said the bear, who was quite enjoying himself. 'If I were a worm I'd crawl all over you.'

Amelia screamed again. 'Don't! I can't bear it. Take them away! Undo

my necklace, quick!'

'Certainly not,' said the sailor doll.

'You wanted to wear it, and you
jolly well can!'

'I'll undo it myself,' said Amelia,
but she couldn't. That knot was tied so
tightly that she couldn't possibly undo
it herself. And nobody else would.

'You can go on wearing worms,'
said the bear. 'Fancy wearing a worm
necklace! Ha, ha! It suits you, Amelia.'

'Please, please do untie the knot,'
begged the big doll. 'Where are the
scissors? We can cut the string.'

But there were no scissors to be
found. The work-basket had gone, and
not one of the toys had any scissors of

their own. So Amelia had to go on wearing her peculiar necklace.

She was very, very miserable. The toys watched the 'worms' growing longer each day, as the roots pushed out from the acorns. 'They're getting bigger, Amelia,' said the bear. 'And longer. And fatter. Oooooh! I wonder if those worms will get hungry, Amelia Jane, and nibble you.'

Amelia sobbed with fright. What could she do? The toy soldier was sorry for her and tried to undo the knot, but he couldn't. 'Go out into the garden and see if the worms will drop down and join the brown worms in the grass,' he said.

So Amelia went out and stood in the garden. And whilst she was there the string, which had got rather wet and rotten at the front of her neck, suddenly broke. And down fell all the acorns, with their funny white roots and tiny shoots.

'They've gone!' yelled Amelia, and fled indoors. The toys went out to see. There lay the acorns, with the white 'worms' sticking out of them.

'Let's bury them in the ground, then perhaps these white worms will go and join their brother brown worms,' said the sailor doll.

So they dug little holes and put the split acorns, with their roots and shoots, carefully in the earth.

And, would you believe it, they all grew into tiny little oak-trees, with strong, white roots delving deep into the ground, and little shoots that bore leaves in the sunshine!

But Amelia Jane didn't know that. She never went near that part of the garden, in case those white worms saw her and went after her.

Poor Amelia! She says she is never going to wear a necklace again, and I don't expect she ever will. The bear says it serves her right – but it really was very funny, wasn't it?

Amelia Jane and the Ink

Amelia Jane was in a very bad mood, and when Tom the toy soldier asked her to play with him, she pushed him away and started to quarrel with him.

'You can't play games,' Amelia Jane shouted. 'You are so stupid.'

'I'm not stupid,' said Tom.

'Yes, you are,' said Amelia Jane.

'Stop it, you two,' said the bear.
'Don't take any notice of Amelia
Jane, Tom.'

'It's difficult not to,' said Tom.

The toys began to talk together,
but they wouldn't talk to Amelia.
When she was in one of her silly
moods, they just took no notice of her.

She didn't like that. 'Be quiet, stop talking,' she said. 'I'm going to write a letter.'

'Well, write it. We don't care!' said the bear. 'Who are you going to write it to?'

'Father Christmas,' said Amelia.

'Well, tell him to come and take you away and put you in his sack, and pop you into a stocking in some other nursery,' said Tom.

Amelia Jane was angry. 'You're unkind,' she said. 'I shall write to him – but I shall ask him to come and take *you* away. So there. You'll be sorry you were nasty to me, then.'

Tom felt rather frightened. He

wasn't at all sure that Father
Christmas might not do what Amelia
said.

'Father Christmas never reads any
letters unless they are written in ink,'
he said at last. He knew Amelia Jane
only had a pencil to write with.

She looked at him. He said it so
loudly that she thought it must be
true. 'All right!' she said. 'I'll write my
letter in ink then!'

The toys stared at her in horror.
Not even the children in the nursery
were allowed to write in ink. Their
mother said they were not old enough.
So the ink was always kept out of
reach on the mantelpiece.

'Amelia Jane! You'd never dare to write in *ink*!' said the bear.

'Wouldn't I?' said Amelia. 'Well, you just see! I shall write my letter in ink, with a pen, and I shall blot it properly and everything.'

'You can't reach the ink,' said the bear.

'I can,' said Amelia.

'You're not to,' said the clockwork clown.

'I just shall then,' said Amelia. She went to the coal-scuttle and climbed up on top of it. From there she climbed on to the top of the nursery fireguard, which went all round the hearth.

Then she leaned on the mantelpiece

to try and reach the bottle of ink. She
just could!

She edged it carefully towards her.
Then she took the bottle into her hands.
'I've got it!' she cried. 'Look!'
She turned to show the toys –
and lost her balance! She fell off the

guard on to the hearth-rug – bump!
The bottle of ink flew into the air and
then fell bang on to Amelia's head. Its
cork shot out and the ink poured all
over Amelia's face! Some went into
her mouth. She spat it out at once.

'Poof! It's horrid!'

The toys stared at Amelia Jane in horror. Her face was blue all over. She did look funny. The toys didn't like her at all. She didn't look like Amelia Jane. She looked rather fierce and wild.

'What's the matter?' said Amelia

Jane, as the toys began to edge away from her.

'We don't like you. You're all blue in the face now,' said the bear.

'As blue as the sailor doll's trousers,' said Tom.

'You frighten me!' squealed the clockwork mouse, and raced into the toy-cupboard as if a cat were after him.

'Don't be silly,' said Amelia, trying to wipe her face with her hand. It made her hand blue. She stared at it and wondered what she looked like. There was a mirror over the book-case. Amelia Jane pushed a chair by the book-case, climbed up it and stood on the top of the book-case. She looked at herself in the mirror there.

'Oh! Oh!' she squealed. 'It isn't me! It isn't me! I'm somebody else! Oh, where have I gone? It isn't me!'

The toys looked at her. Certainly Amelia Jane didn't look like herself at all.

'There's only one thing to do, Amelia,' said Tom. 'You'll have to scrub your face!'

'Yes, I will, I will,' sobbed poor Amelia, taking another look at herself in the mirror, and then scrambling quickly down to the floor. 'Tom, get a scrubbing-brush, quick.'

Tom went to the basin and

climbed up on to the chair below. He knew there was a nail-brush there. He took it and rubbed it on the soap. Then he climbed down and went to Amelia Jane.

'Shall I do the scrubbing?' he asked. Amelia nodded. So Tom began to scrub her face. How he scrubbed!

'The soap's gone in my eye!' yelled Amelia Jane. Tom took no notice.

'Now it's in the other eye!' sobbed Amelia. 'Don't scrub so hard.'

Tom went on scrubbing. 'You're scrubbing my face away,' wailed poor Amelia. 'Don't scrub my nose so hard. Oh, it'll come off, I know it will!'

All the toys stood round, grinning. They couldn't help thinking that it was a very good punishment for Amelia Jane, after quarrelling with Tom so much, and trying to take the ink.

How he scrubbed! Amelia sobbed and cried, and her eyes smarted with the soap, but Tom wouldn't stop until her face was perfectly clean again. All the toys cheered him on. At last his arm ached and he put down the nail-brush.

'There,' he said, 'now you're all right.'

'Thank you,' sobbed Amelia. 'Oh dear, oh dear, why ever did I say I'd write in ink? Look at the mess on the hearthrug!'

Poor Amelia had to set to work and scrub that clean too. She put the empty bottle of ink back on the mantelpiece, feeling very guilty.

'You ought to look in your money-box and put some money by the bottle to pay for some more ink,' said the bear.

So Amelia looked in her money-box and put five coins on the mantelpiece by the bottle. The children found them there the next day, and they *were* surprised!

'Where did this money come from?' they wondered, and they turned to look at the toys. 'Goodness – isn't Amelia's face clean! Whatever has happened to it?'

They might have guessed when they found that their nail-brush was blue with ink – but they didn't!

As for Amelia Jane, she told Tom she was sorry she had quarrelled with him – so one good thing came out of her naughty prank, after all!

Amelia Jane's Boomerang

Amelia Jane found a toy boomerang at the back of the cupboard. Do you know what a boomerang is? It is a bit of curved wood made in such a way that it will always come back to the one who throws it.

You can see the boomerang Amelia Jane found if you look at the picture. She didn't know what it was, at first. Then, when she threw it into the air and found that it came back to her, she was thrilled.

'Now I'll have some fun!' she cried, and she threw the boomerang at the chimneys on the dolls' house! It knocked them off and they slid down the roof, fell to the ground and gave the clockwork mouse a terrible fright.

The boomerang flew back to Amelia Jane, and she caught it. 'Now I'll take off the sailor doll's hat!' she said with a giggle, and threw it again. It neatly took off the sailor doll's hat, and came back to Amelia Jane. She laughed at the sailor doll's look of

surprise when he felt his hat
knocked off.

'Oh, my goodness! Amelia
Jane has found the old boomerang!'
said the bear. 'I hid it away.
Amelia, give it to me.'

Amelia Jane threw the
boomerang at him, and it sliced
off the tip of one of his ears, and
then flew back to the doll. The

bear was very angry.

He ran at Amelia to get the boomerang. But she flung it at him again and he fell over. The boomerang returned to her hand. She laughed excitedly.

'It's no good! I'm *awfully* good with this. If you come rushing at me I'll throw it at you. So keep away. Now watch – I'm going to throw it at the snapdragons in that vase! I'll chop off some of their heads!'

And that's just what she did! The boomerang flew through the air, hit two snapdragons, broke their pretty heads, and then came flying back to the naughty doll.

Amelia Jane had a lovely time that day. She knocked the little china dog off the mantelpiece with her boomerang and he fell on to the hearth and broke a bit off one paw. She threw it at the little mouse who came for crumbs, and he lost two of his whiskers. And she threw it at the railway train and cut the funnel right off.

'How can we stop it?' said the clockwork clown in despair. He had had his hat knocked off six times by the boomerang and now he had stuffed it into his pocket for safety.

'I know where the old pop-gun is,' said the pink cat suddenly. 'Shall we

 get that? It's got a cork on a string, and it always jerks back when it's shot out. You put the cork into the end of the gun, press the trigger – and out shoots the cork. But because it's on a string it always jerks back to the shooter again, like the boomerang goes back to Amelia Jane.'

This was quite a long speech for the pink cat to make, and everyone listened to it, except Amelia Jane, who was trying to knock down a silver thimble left on the mantelpiece.

'Yes! Get the pop-gun!' cried the bear, so the pink cat went to get it. He brought it out of an old box and showed it to the others. Tom the toy soldier fitted the cork into the end. It was on a long string tied to the gun. He pressed the trigger.

POP! Out flew the cork quite fiercely, and hit the bear on the right paw. He gave a yell. 'Don't practise on me, silly! That stung! Practise on Amelia Jane!'

Tom grinned. He went over to Amelia Jane and pointed the pop-gun at the back of her head.

POP! The cork flew out, caught her hair-ribbon, and then jerked back on its string.

Amelia Jane got a terrible shock.

'Oh! What was that?' she cried, and swung round at once.

'We've got a boomerang-cork!' grinned Tom, and shot at her again. POP! The cork hit her on the nose, and she almost fell over.

'Now you stop that!' cried Amelia Jane, 'or I'll throw my boomerang at you!'

'Well, every time you throw your boomerang we're going to shoot you with the pop-gun!' said Tom, putting the cork into the gun again. 'There's no reason why we shouldn't have a bit of fun, too! Look out!'

Pop! The cork hit Amelia Jane right in her middle and she gave a squeal.

'Oh! Oh! You've hit my dinner! Wait till I get that horrid cork! I'll throw it away!'

But she couldn't get the cork because it was tied on with string to the gun, and it always jerked back when it was fired out.

The toys had a wonderful time chasing her round the nursery, popping the cork at her. She didn't have a chance to throw the boomerang at them.

'You're very unkind,' she sobbed as she tried to dodge the toys.

'Oh, no – we're only doing the sort of thing you've been doing,' said Tom. 'You give us your boomerang and we'll give you the pop-gun. Then we can each have a turn at throwing the boomerang too.'

'No,' said Amelia. 'You'd only throw that at me as well. Promise not to and I'll give it to you.'

They promised, and Amelia Jane handed over the boomerang. Tom at once went to hide it away where it would never be found again. But, oh dear, Amelia Jane didn't promise not to shoot at the toys with the pop-gun, and the very first thing she did was to point it at the bear and fire.

POP! It flew out and hit him so hard in his tummy that it made him growl. But she couldn't shoot the cork again because Tom had cut the string and it didn't jerk back to the gun!

'Aha!' said the sailor doll, picking up the loose cork and putting it into his pocket, 'you won't do *that* again, naughty Amelia Jane!

Go and stand in the corner till we say
you can come out. If you don't, we'll
take the gun, tie on the string to the
cork and do a bit of shooting again!'

So Amelia Jane is standing in the
corner, sulking, and I rather think the
toys are going to forget about her for
a very long time!

Amelia Jane and the Scribbles

One day Amelia Jane found a red pencil on the floor. Somebody had dropped it there and forgotten to pick it up. Amelia Jane was pleased.

'Now I can write things in red,' she said. 'Look, this is a pencil that writes in red, toys.'

'Well, if you think you're going to

write in my notebook, you're wrong,' said Tom.

'And if you think I'm going to lend you my little drawing-book to scribble in, you can think again,' said the teddy bear.

'And don't you dare to scribble inside the lid of the brick-box,' said the clockwork clown. 'I spent ages rubbing out some silly scribbles the pink cat did once with a bit of coal.'

'I don't know why you're so sharp with me,' said Amelia Jane. 'Anyone would think I wanted to do something naughty.'

'It's not at all surprising that we should think that,' said the bear.

'You've been fairly good for about a week. That's about as long as you *can* be good for.'

Amelia Jane badly wanted to scribble with her red pencil, but nobody would lend her any paper at all. So she got cross and went inside the toy-cupboard all by herself. When she came out,

she was smiling.

'Now, what's she smiling like that
for?' said Tom, and he went inside the
toy-cupboard. He gave an angry cry,
and the toys went to see why.

'Look!' he said, pointing to the
wall at the back of the cupboard.
'Look what she's done.'

The toys looked. Written across
the wall were lots of words: '*The toy
soldier is silly. The teddy bear is too fat.
The clockwork clown is clumsy. The
clockwork mouse is a baby.*'

'Look at that!' said the clown.
'How disgraceful! Doesn't Amelia
Jane know that no decent people ever
scribble on walls? Only the very lowest

toys do that!'

They went to find Amelia, but they couldn't. But they found something scribbled on the wall near the toy-cupboard, at the bottom:

'*You're all sillies! I shall do what I like, so there! Signed, Amelia Jane.*'

'Isn't she awful?' said the bear. 'Now we shall have to spend ages rubbing this out before anyone sees it. Go and borrow some dusters from the dolls in the dolls' house, Tom.'

But when he got to the dolls' house, he found all the small dolls in a very bad temper.

'Somebody's been in and scribbled over our walls,' said Dinah, the mother doll. 'Look. Someone's written: "*This is a silly dolls' house.*"'

'What a shame,' said the bear. 'That's Amelia Jane. She wants scribbling on herself!'

'That's an awfully good idea of yours, bear,' said the clown. 'If only we could! That would soon stop her silly tricks!'

'Listen,' said the bear, thinking out a plan. 'We're giving a party tomorrow night, aren't we, to all the pixies who live in the garden outside? Well, let's wait till Amelia Jane is asleep tonight, and we'll scribble something across her forehead! She won't know, because she hardly ever looks at herself in the mirror, even to do her hair.'

All the toys giggled. That would be a good joke! They spent quite a lot of time rubbing out the things Amelia Jane had scribbled everywhere, and the big doll peeped out from behind the curtain, and laughed. She didn't know what they were planning for her, or she would have been on her guard.

That night Amelia Jane climbed up into one of the dolls' cots and lay down to sleep. She felt tired. She had done such a lot of writing that day! The toys waited till she was fast asleep, and then Tom climbed up softly to the cot. He sat down gently beside Amelia Jane.

'Pass me the paint-box,' he whispered, and the bear passed it up. A bright red colour was already mixed for him, and the paint-brush was there as well.

Tom began to paint words quickly on Amelia Jane's big smooth forehead. '*This is naughty Amelia Jane*' he put, and tried not to giggle.

Amelia Jane thought it was a fly walking over her head when she felt the paint-brush in her sleep. 'Go away, fly,' she murmured, and that made Tom almost laugh out loud.

He slid down to the floor when he had finished. He wouldn't let the others go up and see what he had done, in case they wakened Amelia Jane. 'Wait till she wakes,' he said. 'Oh, won't it be funny at the party? We shan't need to introduce Amelia Jane to anyone! They'll only have to read what's on her forehead!'

Well, it *was* funny! The pixie guests came along in crowds, longing to dance to the music of the musical-box and to eat the little cakes that Dinah had cooked on the dolls'-house stove. The bear was the host, and he introduced everyone.

But he didn't need to say who Amelia Jane was because as soon as the guests saw her they all giggled and said: 'Oh, this is naughty Amelia Jane!'

Amelia Jane was surprised and cross. She didn't like being called naughty at a party. She frowned and sulked. But as soon as everyone came up to her, the same thing was said: 'Oh, this is naughty Amelia Jane!'

'Why do you say that?' said Amelia, crossly, and she frowned so

hard that she wrinkled up all the red
words on her forehead.

'Don't do that – we can't read
your name!' said a small pixie.
Amelia Jane stared at him.

'What do you mean, you can't
read my name? Of course you can't.
Don't be silly.'

'Oh, now I can,' said the little pixie, when Amelia had stopped frowning. 'Yes – this is naughty Amelia Jane.'

Amelia Jane went to the teddy bear, almost crying. 'Why is everyone horrid to me? Why do they keep saying, "This is naughty Amelia Jane"? Tell me.'

'No,' said the bear.

'Yes,' said Amelia. 'I want to know, please, please, bear.'

'I'll tell you if you promise to give me that red pencil and never to scribble anywhere again,' said the bear. 'It's a low thing to do.'

'All right,' said Amelia Jane, with a

sigh. 'I won't scribble any more. Here's the pencil.'

'Thanks. Now go and look at yourself in the mirror,' said the bear, and Amelia went.

She screamed when she saw the red words on her forehead. 'Oh! Oh, how mean! Now I know why everyone said what they did. I shan't go back to the party.'

So she didn't. She stayed and moped in the toy-cupboard, and that's where the bear found her halfway through. 'Come along,' he said. 'Come and dance.'

'No,' said Amelia. 'Not with this horrid scribble on my forehead.'

The bear took out his hanky. 'Lick it,' he said to Amelia Jane, and she licked his hanky. He rubbed the licky bit over her forehead.

'There!' he said. 'The scribble's gone. Now come along and dance – and mind you behave yourself, or I might write something else on you. You never know!'

So Amelia Jane behaved herself. But I'm afraid her good behaviour won't last long!

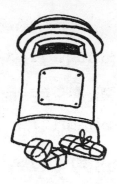

Amelia Jane
Plays Postman

I really must tell you the latest story about Amelia Jane.

On the nursery mantelpiece stood a money-box. It looked exactly like a pillar-box, and it was painted red just like the big ones we post letters in down the road.

But instead of posting letters in

their box the children posted money, of course, and it was a very good way of saving it. 'Clink!' it went when it was dropped in, and the money-box grew heavier and heavier.

Mother kept the key of the box and only unlocked it when the children wanted to take out some money to buy someone a birthday present. She unlocked the box at the bottom then, and the children took the money out.

Now, Amelia Jane suddenly took it into her head that if she found anything left about by the toys she would post it in the red money-box on the mantelpiece! That made the toys very angry indeed.

'Amelia Jane! Have you taken my pink ribbon?' cried the bear.

'Yes. And I've posted it,' said Amelia. 'You are getting very untidy, Teddy, leaving your things about. It will teach you to be tidy.'

Teddy was furious, of course. And so was the clockwork clown when he found that Amelia had actually posted the button that came off his trousers.

'How dare you do that?' he shouted. 'I couldn't help it coming off, could I? I know somebody would have sewn it on again, if you hadn't picked it up and posted it. You're SILLY, Amelia Jane!'

And then she posted the toy soldier's belt! It was a bit tight, so he had undone it and had just put it down while he straightened his trousers a little, when Amelia Jane pounced on it. He was too late to get it back! Into the red money-box it went.

'Now I haven't got a belt!' shouted Tom. 'I look awful.

Stop this nonsense, Amelia Jane, or we'll start posting *your* things in that box!'

'You can't,' said Amelia with a grin. 'I'm the only one that can reach the mantelpiece.'

This was quite true. Amelia Jane was a very big doll and a good climber too. She could reach up to the chair near the fireplace, climb over to the mantelpiece and climb on to that. Then it was easy to post anything in the money-box there.

But none of the other toys could get on to the mantelpiece, so they couldn't possibly post anything belonging to Amelia. It was most

annoying. After she had posted the
baby doll's dear little comb, the toys
held a meeting. Amelia Jane was
asleep in her chair, so she didn't hear
a word.

'We've got to do *some*thing to stop
her,' said the clock. 'She'll be posting
the clockwork mouse's tail next!'

The mouse gave a squeal. 'No, no!
Don't say that! I couldn't bear it.'

'How can we stop her?' wondered
the baby doll.

The teddy bear suddenly slapped
his plump knee.

'I know. I've got an idea!'

'Sh! Don't wake Amelia,' said the
clown.

'Now listen,' said the teddy, excitedly. 'You know next week it's the birthday of the little mouse who lives in the hole in the wall, don't you? Well, listen – ooooh, it's *such* a good idea – you see . . .'

'Oh, do go on! Do tell us!' said the clockwork mouse, impatiently.

'Well – we'll pretend that we are giving the little mouse all sorts of tiny presents, wrapped up in parcels,' said the teddy, grinning. '*But* – we'll put inside the parcels little things belonging to Amelia Jane! We'll put her best hair-ribbon in – and one of her Sunday shoes – and that brooch she likes so much – and her best sash . . .'

'But dear me, we can't *possibly* give her things to the little mouse,' said Tom, shocked. 'That would be quite wrong.'

'Oh, don't you *see* what will happen?' said the teddy. 'Amelia Jane will find the parcels – and she won't be able to stop herself *posting* them – in the money-box! And she'll have posted all her own things and won't be able to get them back!'

There was a silence. Then the toys giggled and thumped Teddy on the back. 'You're marvellous!' they cried. 'It is a simply wonderful idea! We'll do it! Oh, how we'll laugh to see Amelia posting her own things!'

Well, they did just
what they had planned.
They found Amelia's
brooch and wrapped it
up. They found her best
sash, folded it neatly
and wrapped it in paper and tied it
with string. They took her hair-ribbon
and did that up too, and one of her
best shoes! Soon there were four neat
little parcels at the back of the toy-
cupboard.

And, of course, it wasn't long
before Amelia Jane found them. 'Aha!'
she said. 'I suppose these are birthday
parcels for that silly little mouse who
lives in the wall. I'll post them!'

'I warn you not to,' said Tom. 'You'll be sorry if you do, Amelia.'

Amelia laughed and picked up all the parcels. She went towards the fireplace to climb on the chair there.

'You have been warned!' called the clown. But Amelia took no notice at all. Ha – this was a fine trick to play on the toys – to post all the parcels they had got ready for the little mouse!

Thud, thud, thud, thud! Down into the money-box they went, and there they stayed. Amelia Jane climbed down, smiling. 'I have been warned!' she said, mockingly. 'But *I* don't care.'

Nobody said anything. They just waited in patience till Amelia wanted her brooch or her ribbon or sash. She soon did, because she was to go to a party given by the doll in the next house. The children were taking her.

'I shall wear my best shoes, my sash, my blue hair-ribbon, and my brooch,' she said. 'I *shall* look grand!'

But she couldn't find them, though she hunted everywhere. She turned to the watching toys. 'You know something about them!' she cried. 'What have you done with them?'

'Nothing – except just wrap them up into neat little parcels!' grinned the clown.

'But what for? Oh, *what's* happened to my precious, precious things?' groaned Amelia.

'You should know,' said the bear. 'You picked up all the parcels yesterday.'

'You p-p-p-posted them!' squealed the clockwork mouse, stammering in excitement, and then going off into a fit of giggles.

'I *posted* them!' said Amelia. 'What do you mean? Those were birthday parcels for the mouse, weren't they? Oh, oh, oh – why didn't you tell me what they were?'

'We warned you, we did warn you not to post them,' said the clown, and

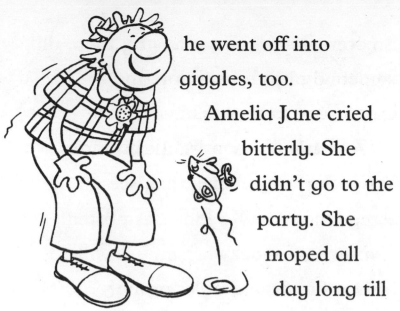

he went off into
giggles, too.

Amelia Jane cried
bitterly. She
didn't go to the
party. She
moped all
day long till
the toys felt quite sorry for her. Then
she dried her eyes.

'I'm sorry I posted everybody's
things,' she said. 'I know what it feels
like now to lose my things in that
money-box. I'll find the key, undo the
box and get everything out.'

But she couldn't find the key
because Mother had it in her purse.

So everything has got to stay there till somebody has a birthday and the money-box is unlocked.

And *what* a surprise the children are going to get when they see all the things that Amelia Jane has posted! I'm sure the clockwork mouse will have a fit of the giggles again!

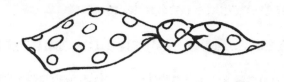

Amelia Jane is Naughty Again

Listen to what Amelia Jane did a little while ago – she's almost as rascally as Brer Rabbit sometimes!

It all happened when a new toy came to stay in the nursery. He really belonged to the children's cousin, but she was going away and asked her cousins to look after this toy for her.

He was rather a peculiar-looking toy. He was made of wood, and he had jointed legs and arms and hands – and even toes. He was dressed like a gardener, with a green baize apron in front, a scarf round his neck, and rolled-up sleeves that showed his jointed arms.

The peculiar thing about him was his head. It could nod up and down and shake from side to side because it was on a kind of spring. It was very surprising to the toys to see somebody that could nod his head or shake it like that.

'What's your name?' asked Amelia Jane. 'Do we call you Mr Noddy or Mr Shaky?'

'I've got a cousin called Mr Shaky,' said the wooden man. 'I'm called Mr Up-and-To.'

'What a peculiar name!' said the sailor doll.

'Not really,' said the wooden man. 'Just a mixture of *Up*-and-Down and *To*-and-Fro – Mr Up-and-To.'

'Why not Mr Fro-and-Down?' asked Amelia Jane, and went off into giggles.

'How clever you are!' said Mr Up-

and-To, admiringly. 'That's a *much* nicer name! Really, I think you are a very clever doll.'

'Oh, I am,' said Amelia Jane at once. 'Aren't I, toys? If anything goes wrong, ask me how to put it right! If you want to know anything, ask me! If you –'

'That's enough, Amelia Jane,' said Tom. 'Stop blowing your own trumpet.'

'Oh, can she blow a trumpet, too?' said Mr Up-and-To, surprised. 'Well, well – if that isn't cleverer still. My mouth's too wooden to hold a trumpet.'

'Amelia's mouth is big enough to

hold a dozen trumpets, if she wanted to blow them about herself,' said the bear.

'Don't be unkind,' said Amelia Jane. 'You know I'm very clever.'

'I know you're very, very naughty,' said the bear. 'Now, you leave Mr Up-and-To alone, and don't stuff him up with any more tales.'

But Amelia Jane wouldn't leave the little wooden man alone. For one thing, he really was very, very stupid, and he believed every word anyone said. Amelia Jane found that out at once, and, oh, the tricks she played on that poor wooden man!

'Don't go near the brick-box,' she

would say. 'It's Monday today, and there might be a snake there!'

And, will you believe it, Mr Up-and-To would keep right the other side of the nursery, afraid that a snake might spring out at him.

'Don't go too near the Noah's Ark today, because it's Friday,' Amelia would say next. 'The lions are always so fierce on Friday.'

Mr Up-and-To didn't go near the Noah's Ark all day long. He asked Amelia Jane why the lions were so fierce on Fridays.

'Well, I expect that's the day they're fed at the Zoo,' said Amelia Jane, and the poor stupid little wooden man thought that was a very good reason.

'You're bad, Amelia Jane,' said Tom. 'Stuffing him up with tales like that. Whatever will you say next?'

'Aha! You wait and see!' said Amelia. And she went and whispered in Mr Up-and-To's big wooden ear.

'Don't go near the toy soldier today because it's Saturday and he might bite you.'

Poor Mr Up-and-To! He ran away as soon as Tom came near, and as Amelia Jane had given Tom a sweet to take to the wooden man, he kept on trying to find him, so that he could give him the sweet.

'I can't *think* why the wooden man keeps rushing off as soon as he sees me,' said Tom, surprised.

'It's Saturday and he doesn't like soldiers on Saturday,' said Amelia Jane, wickedly.

'Don't be silly,' said Tom. 'Here, take your sweet back. I'm not going

to rush after Mr Up-and-To all day long. You've told him something about me. I know you!'

Now one day Amelia Jane put a knot into her little blue hanky to remind her not to forget to mend her dress. Mr Up-and-To saw her knotting the knot, and he was most interested.

'What's that for?' he asked.

'Well, most people put a knot into their hanky if they want to remember something,' said Amelia. 'This knot says to me: "Mend your dress tonight, Amelia Jane." And I shall.'

'Very, very clever,' said the wooden man. 'I think I shall do that too,

Amelia. I'm always forgetting things, aren't I?'

'Well, you just try putting knots into your hanky, and you will soon have a marvellous memory,' said Amelia Jane.

So the next time Mr Up-and-To wanted to remember something, he took out his big, red-spotted hanky and tied a very large knot in it.

'That's to tell me to remember to clean my shoes tonight,' he said to himself. But, of course, when he saw the knot again he couldn't for the life of him remember what he had put it into his hanky for.

I'll ask Amelia Jane, he thought.

She always knows everything. So he went to find the big doll.

'Amelia,' he said, 'supposing I forgot what I had put a knot in my hanky for, would you be able to tell me?'

'Of course!' said Amelia, with a very wicked grin.

'Well, what's this knot for?' asked the wooden man, and he showed her the very big knot.

'Oh – that's to remind you to climb up to the basin-taps with a jug from the dolls' house, fill it with water, and give me a drink,' said Amelia at once.

'Is it really?' said the wooden man, in surprise. 'Well, fancy me forgetting that! I'll go at once, Amelia Jane.'

So, much to the toys' amazement, he got a jug, climbed all the way up to the basin, and held the jug under the tap-drips till he got it full. Then he gave Amelia Jane a drink.

'Well! He must be very fond of her,' said the clockwork clown, in surprise. 'Fancy doing all that for *Amelia*!'

Amelia was pleased. Her naughty mind began to work hard – and the very next time Mr Up-and-To was asleep she crept up to him, took his hanky from his pocket and made a very big knot there!

So, of course, the next time he took it out another knot stared him in the face. What *could* it be for?

'Oh, that?' said Amelia Jane. 'Dear, dear, have you forgotten already why you put it there, Mr Up-and-To? Why, it was to remind you to go to the toy sweet shop and bring me six of those tiny pink sweets.'

'Dear me – was it really?' said Mr Up-and-To, puzzled. 'I simply can't remember that at all! But I'll go at once, Amelia Jane.'

So he solemnly went to the toy-shop and took six of the little pink

sweets from a bottle and gave them to
Amelia Jane. She popped them all
into her mouth at once.

Tom and the bear came over in a
hurry. They spoke very sternly to Mr
Up-and-To.

'Look here! That's stealing. Those
sweets belong to the children, not to
us. How dare you! Put them back!'

'He can't,' said Amelia, speaking
with her mouth full. 'I'm eating them.'

'Did she tell you to get them?' the
bear asked the wooden man.

'Well, no – not exactly. I – er – I
put a knot in my hanky to remember
to get them,' said Mr Up-and-To. 'I
must say I'm very surprised at myself

for putting a knot there to remind me of that. I'm very, very sorry, Teddy.'

Amelia Jane giggled to herself. She felt very naughty indeed, with a nice stupid fellow like Mr Up-and-To to play tricks on.

She put more knots in his hanky, and when he asked her what they could possibly be for she told him all sorts of things.

'That knot you put there is to remind you to get me the little blue brooch you'll find in a box at the back of the toy-cupboard,' she said. It belonged to the baby doll, and it was very bad of Amelia Jane to get the wooden man to fetch it for her.

'And that knot's to remind you to get me some cakes from the dolls'-house kitchen,' said Amelia another time. 'They've been baking today. And look, there's a little tiny knot in this corner of your hanky – that's to tell you to remember to have a cake for yourself, too.'

And, dear me, there were Amelia Jane and the wooden man both eating cakes together!

The toys were very, very angry, and the dolls'-house dolls threatened to fetch a policeman.

'If you tell Mr Up-and-To any more naughty things to do, we'll punish you, Amelia Jane,' said the bear. 'Oh, we know it's you all right! He's too stupid to think of these things himself. You put them into his head.'

Amelia got cross. She put *four* knots in Mr Up-and-To's hanky at once. He ran to her, most surprised, when he discovered them. 'Amelia Jane! Look here – I've put *four* knots this time. Whatever can they be for?'

'This one's to remind you to pull the toy soldier's nose, and this one's to remind you to tread on the tail of the clockwork mouse, and that's to tell you to be sure and pinch the teddy bear, and that's to remind you to run off with the clown's key,' said Amelia Jane.

Well, the wooden man was most astonished at himself. To think he had decided to do all those things and had actually put knots in his hanky to remind him. Well, well – he'd better start off with the toy soldier. He would pull his nose.

He tried to, but Tom caught his wooden hands, and stopped him.

'Listen, Mr Up-and-To,' he said sternly. 'What's up with you? You *seem* so gentle and good, and a bit stupid – and yet you do all kinds of very, very naughty things. Why?'

'It's the knots in my hanky,' explained the wooden man sadly. 'Amelia Jane always tells me what they're for, you see. She knows.'

The toys went off to the back of the toy-cupboard to have a meeting. So *that's* what Amelia Jane was doing!

'She puts the knots in the hanky when the old wooden man is asleep,' said Teddy. 'And then when he asks her what he's put them there for, she tells him all kinds of nonsense. Well – *I'm* going to tell him what his next knot is for!'

The toys grinned. They could guess what the bear was going to tell Mr Up-and-To.

It was the bear that night who put a knot into the wooden man's hanky. It was such an enormous knot that the hanky seemed all knot when he had finished!

Mr Up-and-To was astonished to see such a big knot when he woke up. The bear was just nearby, so instead of asking Amelia Jane he showed the knot to Teddy.

'Look at that!' he said. 'A tremendous knot. Something *most* important to remember. I'd better ask Amelia Jane what it is for.'

'No, don't,' said the bear. 'She wouldn't dream of telling you what the knot's for. Ask me – or the toy soldier – or the clown. We all know. We'll tell you all right.'

'Tell me then,' said the wooden man.

'That knot, that very large knot, is to remind you to be sure and give Amelia Jane a good scolding,' said the bear. 'Don't look so surprised. That's what the knot is there for. Isn't it, Tom? Isn't it, everyone?'

And all the toys nodded and said yes, that was what the very large knot meant.

'She's been bad to you,' said

Teddy. 'She's tried to make you bad, too. She must be punished – and you are the one to punish her, Mr Up-and-To. Go now.'

So he's gone to find Amelia Jane, feeling very cross indeed. She tried to make him bad, did she? Mr Up-and-To didn't want to be bad. He'd give Amelia Jane a good scolding!

She's hiding, of course. But the wooden man will find her. He's very, very determined once he makes his mind up – and sooner or later there'll be howls from the nursery, I'm sure of that.

I don't feel a bit sorry, and neither does anyone else. Amelia Jane has

had her fun, and now, alas, she's got
to pay for it!

Amelia Jane Goes Up the Tree

It was springtime, and the birds were all nesting. Amelia Jane was most excited.

'The birds are building their nests,' she said. 'They are laying eggs.'

'Well, they do that every year,' said Tom.

'I want to make a collection of

birds' eggs,' said Amelia Jane, grandly.

'You naughty doll!' said the clockwork clown. 'You know quite well you mustn't take birds' eggs.'

'Well, I don't see why birds can't spare me one or two of their eggs,' said Amelia. 'After all – they can't count.'

'Amelia Jane, you know quite well that birds get dreadfully upset if they see anyone near their nests,' said the teddy bear. 'You know that sometimes they get very frightened, and they desert their nests – leave them altogether – so that the eggs get cold, and never hatch out.'

'Oh, don't lecture me so!' said Amelia Jane. 'I said I wanted to make a collection of birds' eggs, and so I am going to. You can't stop me.'

'You are a very bad doll,' said the clown, and he turned his back on Amelia. 'I don't like you one bit.'

Amelia Jane laughed. She was feeling in a very naughty mood. She looked out of the window, down into a big chestnut tree. In the fork of a branch was a nest. It belonged to a thrush.

'There's a thrush's nest just down there,' said Amelia. 'I wish I could climb down. But I can't. It's too dangerous. Perhaps I could climb up.'

'How could you do that?' said the curly-haired doll, in a scornful voice. 'Don't be silly. None of us could climb up that tall trunk!'

But the next day Amelia Jane was excited. 'The gardener has put a ladder up the chestnut tree!' she said. 'He has, really. He is cutting off some of the bigger branches, because they knock against the low roof of the shed. I shall slip down, wait till the gardener has gone to his dinner, and then climb the ladder!'

'Amelia Jane! You don't mean to say you really *are* going to rob a bird's nest!' cried the clown.

'Oh yes,' said Amelia. 'Why

should the bird mind if one or two eggs are taken? She will probably be glad that she hasn't so many hungry beaks to fill, when the eggs hatch out!'

So, to the horror of the watching toys, Amelia Jane slipped downstairs, out of the garden door and up to the ladder, as soon as the gardener had gone to his dinner.

The toys all pressed their noses to the window and watched her.

'She's climbing the ladder!' said the clown. 'She really is!'

'She's up to the top of it!' squeaked the clockwork mouse.

'She's going right into the tree!' cried the teddy bear, and he almost

broke the window with
his nose, he pressed so
hard against it.

Amelia Jane was climbing
the tree very well. She was a big
strong doll, and she swung herself up
easily. She soon came to the big
thrush's nest. The
mother-thrush was
not there.

I suppose she has
gone to stretch her
wings a little, thought
Amelia Jane. She
stretched out her hand
and put it into the nest.
There were four eggs there,

and they felt smooth and warm.
Amelia Jane took one and put it into
the pocket of her red dress. Then she
took another, and put that in her
second pocket.

'There!' she said. 'Two will be
enough, I think. I can start a very nice
collection with two. How pretty they
are! I like them.'

She sat up in the tree for a little
while, enjoying the sound of the wind
in the leaves and liking the swaying of
the bough she sat on. It was so
exciting.

'I'd better go back now,' she said.
'I don't want to be here when the
mother-thrush comes back.'

So she began to climb
down the tree again.
But, after a while, she
heard a noise. It was
someone whistling.
She peeped down
between the
leaves.

'It's the
gardener!'
said Amelia
Jane in dismay.

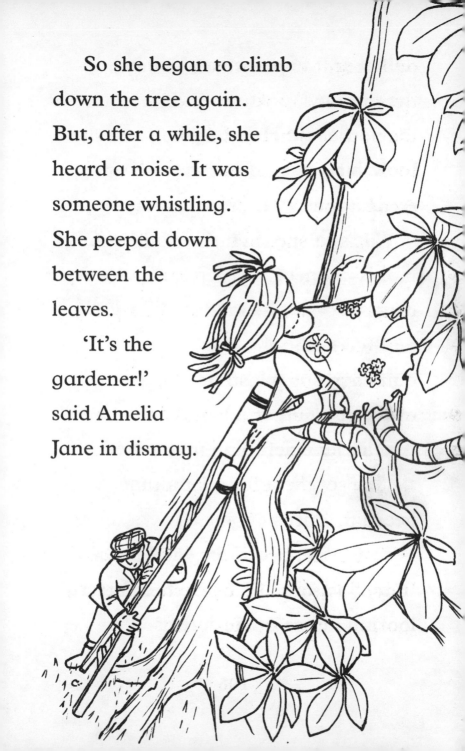

'Oh dear, I hope he isn't coming up the tree now.'

He wasn't. He was doing something else – something that filled Amelia Jane with great dismay.

'He's taking away the ladder! Oh my! It's gone! However am I to get down again? The ladder's gone!'

It certainly *was* gone. The gardener, still whistling, carried it away for another job. And there was Amelia Jane, left high up the tree!

She sat there for a long time. She heard the thrush come back again to her nest. She heard the wind in the trees. She saw the toys in the nursery looking out at her in surprise, wondering why she didn't climb down and come back.

'I do feel lonely and frightened,' said Amelia to herself, when the day went and the cold night began to come. 'I shall be very afraid up here in the dark. Oh dear, why ever did I think of climbing the tree and stealing eggs? It's a punishment for me, it really is!'

She began to cry. And when Amelia Jane cried she made a noise. She sobbed and gulped and howled. It was a dreadful noise.

A small pixie, who lived in the primrose bed below, heard the noise and wondered what it was. So she flew up into the tree to see.

'Oh, it's you, Amelia Jane,' said
the pixie. 'What's the matter? You're
keeping me awake with that dreadful
noise.'

'I can't get down,' sobbed Amelia.
'I want to get back to the nursery,
and I can't.'

'Whatever made you climb up?'
asked the pixie. But Amelia was too
ashamed to tell her.

'Please help me,' begged the big
doll. 'I am so unhappy.'

'Well, maybe the thrush who lives
higher up the tree can help you,' said
the pixie, and she flew up to see.
Amelia Jane felt most uncomfortable.

She had taken eggs from the thrush's nest. Oh dear! How she wished she hadn't!

The pixie flew back again, and the big brown thrush was with her.

'Here's the thrush,' said the pixie. 'She is very sad and unhappy tonight, because some horrid person stole two of her precious eggs, but she is very kind, and although she is sad she will help you.'

'Yes, I will help you, help you, help you,' sang the thrush sweetly. 'I am sad, sad, sad, but I will help you, big, big doll.'

'How can you help me?' asked Amelia in surprise.

'I can guide you right up the tree,' said the thrush. 'I know the way. I can bring you right up to the nursery window-sill, and you can knock on the window and get the toys to let you in. Then you will be safe, safe, safe!'

'Oh, you *are* kind!' said Amelia Jane. She turned to follow the thrush up the tree.

'Hold on to one of my tail-feathers,' said the thrush kindly. 'Don't be afraid of pulling it out.'

Amelia held on to a feather, and

the thrush guided her gently up the dark tree. After a little while she stopped and spoke.

'Big doll, can you see my nest just here? It is such a nice, comfortable one. It is very dark now, but perhaps you can just see two eggs gleaming in the cup. Aren't they lovely?'

Amelia Jane could see them gleaming in the half-darkness. The thrush went on, half speaking, half singing.

'You know, I had more eggs than those you see. But whilst I was away this morning someone took two, took two, took two. It nearly broke my heart. Now I shall only have two children instead of four. Can you imagine anyone bad enough to steal from a little bird like me?'

Amelia Jane felt the two eggs in her pockets, and she began to sob. 'What's the matter?' asked the kindly thrush; and she pressed her warm, feathery body close to Amelia to comfort her.

'Oh, brown thrush, oh, brown thrush,' sobbed Amelia. 'I took your eggs. I've got them in my pockets. Let me put them back into your nest, please, please! They are still lovely and warm, and I haven't broken them. I'm the horrid person that took them, but I'm dreadfully sorry now!'

She took the warm eggs from her
pockets and put them gently into the
nest.

'Now push me down the tree; do
anything you like to punish me!' said
Amelia Jane. 'I know I deserve it.'

'What a foolish doll you are!' said the thrush, very happy to see her eggs once more. 'Because you were unkind to me is no reason why I should now be unkind to you. I am happy again, so I want to make you happy, too! Come along, hold on to my tail-feather, and we'll go higher till we come to the window-sill!'

So up they went, with Amelia wiping her eyes on her skirt every now and again because she was so ashamed of herself and so grateful to the thrush for forgiving her and being kind to her.

They came to the window-sill, and Amelia rapped on it. The teddy bear, who was just the other side, called the clown, and together they opened the window. Amelia slipped inside. She said goodbye to the thrush, and then looked at the toys.

'Whatever happened to you?' said the clown. 'Did you take the eggs? Surely that was the thrush helping you just now!'

'I did take the eggs, but I've given them back, and I'm ashamed of myself for taking them,' said Amelia in a very small voice. 'I shall never, never do such a thing again in my life. I'm going to be a Good Doll now.'

'Hmmm,' said the clown. 'We've

heard that before, Amelia Jane! We'll see what the thrush has to say tomorrow!'

I heard her singing the next day, and do you know what she sang? She sang: 'Took two, took two, put them back, put them back, put them back, sweet, sweet, sweet!' Listen, and maybe you'll hear her singing that, too!

She's big! She's bad!

She's the terror of the toy cupboard... and she's back!

More adventures from Amelia Jane.

 EGMONT

 EGMONT